Nana's Garden
Sophy Williams

VIKING

One day in early autumn, Thomas
was going out to play.

"You come too, Nana," he said.

"Me?" said Nana. "I'm too old
to play."

"I wish you weren't," said
Thomas.

The sun cast shadows in Nana's garden. Thomas kicked up the leaves, still wet from the morning's rain. A branch cracked, an apple fell.

"Who's there?" said Thomas.

The wind in the trees murmured, *"It's only me. An echo, a whisper, a heartbeat."*

The air grew cold in Nana's garden. Thomas turned and looked around. The long grass was flattened as if someone had been walking there. A trail of footsteps seemed to run in and out of the trees. Thomas followed them, all around the orchard and across the lawn to Nana's shed.

Thomas had never been inside, but now he thought perhaps there was something precious hidden there.

As he reached up to open the door, he thought he saw someone watching him.

"Who's there?" he said.

The wind whistled under the door. *"Inside,"* it said. *"Inside."*

A pale light shone through the little window, and lit up the muddle inside. Thomas began to search. Through the ancient chest of drawers, behind an old mirror, inside a box of rusty tools. Then at the back of the shed Thomas found a tall cupboard. He opened the door. Dust flew up in a cloud. Spiders and mice scuttled. From a dark corner, a worn, friendly face looked out at him.

Very gently, very carefully, Thomas lifted out the treasure.

At the window, the small fingers of another child gripped the sill. There was a shimmer of blue, a wisp of hair, a bright eye watching.

"There, there," sang the other child. *"He's been waiting, all these long years."*

Thomas hugged the treasure and took it outside. As he sat on the damp grass he felt a tap on his shoulder.

"Hello."

"Hello," said Thomas. "Who are you? This is Nana's garden."

"It's my garden too," said the other child. *"I've come for Joshua."*

"But I found him," said Thomas.

"I know," she said. *"But he's mine."*

The wind was very still. Thomas looked at the little girl. "Let's play," he said.

They played with Joshua.
They played I-spy and giant's
footsteps. They played statues and
hide-and-seek. The sun came out.

They raced in and out of the trees — all around the orchard and up the steps.

"*Come on,*" said the other child. "*I'll show you the secret places.*"

They ran through Nana's garden to the wild part where Thomas had never been before. Brambles caught at their clothes, leaves crunched under their feet.

"Look, Thomas," said the other child. *"This is where Josie and Tsar are buried. Josie was a big sad labrador. Tsar was a snappy little terrier. He pined for days when Josie died. He didn't last long after."*

"And see that rose over there," said the child. *"I planted it because my name is Rose."*

"Nana's name is Rose too," said Thomas.

The light began to fade in Nana's garden.

"I'm tired now," said Rose. *"I've got to go."*

"Don't go," said Thomas. "Stay with me."

"I am with you," she said. *"I'm always with you."*

"Please don't go," said Thomas again.

But Rose was already
through the gate.
Thomas ran after her.
"Here, take Joshua," he
said. "He's yours."

Then the light was gone in Nana's garden. There was no one there. Just an echo, a shadow, a heartbeat.

Thomas ran back inside and
hugged his grandmother fiercely.
"I love you, Nana," he said.

For Poppy, Daniel, Jasmin and Ruthie

VIKING

Published by the Penguin Group
Penguin Books USA Inc., 375 Hudson Street, New York, New York 10014, U.S.A.
Penguin Books Ltd, 27 Wrights Lane, London W8 5TZ, England
Penguin Books Australia Ltd, Ringwood, Victoria, Australia
Penguin Books Canada Ltd, 10 Alcorn Avenue, Toronto, Ontario, Canada M4V 3B2
Penguin Books (N.Z.) Ltd, 182–190 Wairau Road, Auckland 10, New Zealand

Penguin Books Ltd, Registered Offices: Harmondsworth, Middlesex, England

First published in Great Britain by Hutchinson Children's Books,
an imprint of Random House UK Limited, 1993
First American edition published by Viking,
a division of Penguin Books USA Inc., 1994

1 3 5 7 9 10 8 6 4 2

Copyright © Sophy Williams 1993
All rights reserved

Library of Congress Catalog Card Number: 93–60571
ISBN 0–670–85287–2
Printed in Singapore   Set in Bembo